To my sister, Barbie, and to Winthrop, a parrot who loves pizza
—C.S.

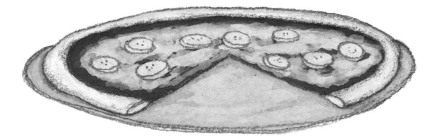

Text and illustrations © 1994 by Catherine Siracusa.
All rights reserved.
Printed in Singapore.
For more information address Hyperion Books for Children,
114 Fifth Avenue, New York NY 10011.

FIRST EDITION
1 3 5 7 9 10 8 6 4 2

Library of Congress Cataloging-in-Publication Data

Siracusa, Catherine.
The Parrot Problem / Catherine Siracusa—1st ed.
p.   cm.
Summary: While Gina watches Pepperoni the parrot for Aunt Sophia,
the bird escapes and causes havoc in the neighborhood.
ISBN 1-56282-626-3 (trade)—ISBN 1-56282-627-1 (lib. bdg.)
[1. Parrots—Fiction.] I. Title. PZ7.S6215Par 1994 [E]—dc20 93-23334 CIP AC

The artwork for each picture is prepared using gouache, watercolor, pencil, and colored pencil.

This book is set in 17 pt. Baskerville.

The PARROT PROBLEM

CATHERINE SIRACUSA

Hyperion Books for Children
New York

A big yellow taxi stopped

in front of Gina's house.

"Mom! Aunt Sophia is here!"

said Gina.

"Hello, Gina," said Aunt Sophia.

"Hello, Gina,"

said a bright green parrot in a cage.

"Hello, Pepperoni!" said Gina.

"Hello! Hello! Hello!"

said Pepperoni the parrot.

"Welcome, Sophia," said Mom.

"Come inside."

"Let me out!" said Pepperoni.

"Out! Out! Out!"

Aunt Sophia opened his cage.

Pepperoni stepped onto her finger.

"BANANA!" said Pepperoni.

"He is hungry," said Aunt Sophia.

Gina ran to the kitchen

and came back with a banana.

Pepperoni flew onto Gina's shoulder.

She gave him a piece of banana.

"BANANA! BANANA!" said Pepperoni.

"Pepperoni likes bananas," said Mom.

"Yes, he does," said Aunt Sophia.

"But Gina knows what Pepperoni

likes to eat best of all."

"Pizza!" said Gina.

"PIZZA! PIZZA! PIZZA!"
said Pepperoni.
"Calm down, Pepperoni,"
said Aunt Sophia.

"Maybe we will order a pizza
from Cousin Tony for lunch,"
said Mom.
"Hooray!" said Gina.
"Hooray! Hooray!" said Pepperoni.

Aunt Sophia yawned.

"It was a long trip," she said.

"Why don't you take a little nap?"
said Mom.

"I will watch Pepperoni,"
said Gina.

Gina put Pepperoni back in his cage.

"Have fun," said Aunt Sophia.

"I will see you later."

Pepperoni swung back and forth
on the swing in his cage.

"I have a swing, too," said Gina.

"I will show you my swing.
Okay?"

"Okay! Okay!" said Pepperoni.

Gina carried Pepperoni's cage
into the backyard.

Gina swung back and forth
on her swing.
Pepperoni swung back and forth
on the swing in his cage.
"I love to swing!" said Gina.
"Swing! Swing! Swing!" said Pepperoni.

"Let me out!" said Pepperoni.

"Out! Out! Out!"

"You can swing with me," said Gina.

She opened the cage.

Pepperoni climbed onto her shoulder.

They swung back and forth

on Gina's swing.

Suddenly a big orange cat ran
toward Pepperoni.
"SQUAWK!" said Pepperoni.
And he flew out of the yard.
"Bad kitty!" cried Gina.
"Pepperoni, come back!"

Gina ran out of the yard.

"Pepperoni, where are you?" she said.

She ran to the corner.

"PEPPERONI! PEPPERONI!" she shouted.

"Gina, you do not have to shout,"
said Mario, the grocer.

"I have plenty of pepperoni
in the store."

"Mario, I do not want
that kind of pepperoni," said Gina.

"Pepperoni is a parrot.
Have you seen him?"

"A bright green parrot just stole
one of my bananas," said Mario.

"That was Pepperoni!" cried Gina.

"Which way did he go?"

"He flew into the park," said Mario.

"That bird should be in a cage!"

"I am sorry about the banana,"
said Gina.

Gina ran to the park.

She saw a banana peel on the ground.

"Pepperoni was here!" she said.

Gina looked all around the park.

"Pepperoni is gone," she said.

"What will I tell Aunt Sophia?"

Gina sat down on a park bench.

"What can I do now?"

Then she looked across the street.

Gina saw a small crowd

in front of Valenti's drugstore.

Pepperoni sat on the drugstore sign.

"There is Pepperoni!" said Gina.

Gina ran across the street.

"Pepperoni, come down!" she said.

"You are a bad bird!"

"I am a good bird! I am a good bird!"
said Pepperoni.

"He talks!" said Mrs. Valenti,
the druggist.

"Talk! Talk! Talk!" said Pepperoni.

And he flew into the dentist's office
on the second floor.

"Get this parrot out of here!"
cried Dr. Como, the dentist.

"Out! Out! Out!" said Pepperoni.

And he flew back into the park.

"Pepperoni, come back!" said Gina.

"I will call the police," said Dr. Como.

"That bird should be in jail!"

"I will call the fire department,"
said Mrs. Valenti.

"They will know what to do."

Everyone ran to the park.

Pepperoni sat on top of the flagpole.

"PEPPERONI!" shouted Gina.

"PEPPERONI! PEPPERONI!"

said the crowd.

But Pepperoni would not come down.

Just then a police car drove
into the park.

"WHERE IS THE PARROT PROBLEM?"
shouted Officer Neal and Officer Barbie.

"NO PROBLEM! NO PROBLEM!"
said Pepperoni.

And he flew to the top
of a streetlight.

"Follow that parrot!"

said Officer Neal.

"Please be careful," said Gina.

"Do not worry," said Officer Barbie.

"We can get him down."

Officer Barbie climbed
onto Officer Neal's shoulders.
She reached out to Pepperoni.
"Come here, you bad bird," she said.
"I am a good bird! I am a good bird!"
said Pepperoni.
Then he grabbed Officer Barbie's hat,
and he flew to the top of a big statue.

"Stop, thief!" cried Officer Barbie.

"Hold still, Barbie!"

said Officer Neal.

"Help!" said Officer Barbie.

Suddenly they both fell backward,

right into the goldfish pond!

"I am soaking wet!"

cried Officer Barbie.

"Arrest that parrot!"

said Officer Neal.

"Pepperoni,
come down!"
said Gina.

A big red fire truck
drove into the park.
"Where is the parrot problem?"
said Fireman Pete and Fireman Phil.
"Do not say that," said Gina.
"You will scare Pepperoni."

"Watch out for that parrot,"
said Officer Neal.
"He is a troublemaker,"
said Officer Barbie.

"We can get him down,"
said Fireman Pete.
"No problem," said Fireman Phil.

Fireman Pete held the ladder.

Fireman Phil climbed up to Pepperoni.

"Hello, birdie," said Fireman Phil.

"Hello! Hello! Hello!"
said Pepperoni.

"Get that bird!" said Fireman Pete.

"Let's go, Pepperoni,"

said Fireman Phil.

"Okay?"

"Okay! Okay!" said Pepperoni.

He stepped onto the fireman's finger.

"Good birdie," said Fireman Phil.

"I am a good bird," said Pepperoni.

"DON'T FORGET MY HAT!"

shouted Officer Barbie.

"Forget it! Forget it!"

said Pepperoni.

And he flew off of Fireman Phil's finger.

Fireman Phil tried to catch Pepperoni.

But he reached too far.

Now Fireman Phil was hanging

from the statue's arm.

"Help!" he cried.

"Hang on, Phil!" said Fireman Pete.

"We will help you!"

said Officer Barbie and Officer Neal.

They ran toward Fireman Pete.
But Officer Neal slipped
on the banana peel,
and they all fell down.

"I cannot hold on much longer!"
said Fireman Phil.
Fireman Pete got the net
from the fire truck.
"Let go, Phil!" he said.
"We will catch you!"

Fireman Phil fell into the net.

"Hooray!" said the crowd.

"Are you okay?" said Fireman Pete.

"I am okay," said Fireman Phil.

"But where is Pepperoni?"

"There he is!" said Gina.

Pepperoni sat on top of the flagpole.

"Now what do we do?"
asked Officer Neal.

"I wish we had some birdseed,"
said Fireman Pete.

"I have a better idea," said Gina.

"I will be right back."

Gina ran across the park.

"Gina, did you catch that parrot?"
asked Mario, the grocer.

"Not yet," said Gina.

"Take these bananas," said Mario.

"That parrot loves my bananas."

"Thanks, Mario!" said Gina.

Gina ran to Cousin Tony's
pizza parlor.

"Cousin Tony! I need a pizza
for Pepperoni!" said Gina.

"One pepperoni pizza coming up!"
said Tony.

"No!" said Gina. "I need a pizza
for Pepperoni the parrot!"

"Aunt Sophia's parrot?" said Tony.

"Yes," said Gina.

"I have to catch him!"

"What kind of pizza does he like?"
asked Tony.

"Salami and eggplant?
Mushroom and meatball?"

Gina held up Mario's bananas.

"A *banana* pizza?" said Tony.

"I have never made one of those."

"Pepperoni will love it,"
said Gina.

"Okay. I will do it!" said Tony.

He quickly made the banana pizza.

Soon it was ready.

"Let's go, Gina," said Tony.

They hurried to the park.

Pepperoni still sat on the flagpole.

"Pepperoni!" called Gina.

"Come down for pizza!"

"PIZZA! PIZZA! PIZZA!"

said Pepperoni.

But he would not come down.

"IT IS A BANANA PIZZA!" shouted Gina.

Pepperoni flew off of the flagpole

and landed on Gina's shoulder.

He tasted the banana pizza.

"Very tasty!" said Pepperoni.

"He likes it!" said Tony.

"I never heard of a banana pizza,"
said Fireman Phil.

"Yuck!" said Officer Neal.

"Maybe it is good,"
said Officer Barbie.

"May we have a taste?"
said Fireman Pete.

"Sure!" said Tony. "It is the greatest!"

Everyone crowded around Tony
to taste the banana pizza.
"It is the greatest!" they said.
"Let's go home, Pepperoni," said Gina.
"Thanks, everyone! Good-bye!"
"Bye-bye!" said Pepperoni.

Gina walked home very slowly.

Pepperoni sat on her shoulder.

They went into her house.

"Hello, Gina!" said Aunt Sophia.

"I had a nice nap.

Did you and Pepperoni have fun?"

"Fun! Fun! Fun!" said Pepperoni.

"I just called Cousin Tony," said Mom.

"I ordered a very special pizza

for lunch."

"What kind of pizza?" asked Gina.

"A banana pizza," said Mom.

"Oh no!" said Gina.

"What is wrong?" said Aunt Sophia.

"Tony says it is very good."

"It *is* good," said Gina.

"Just ask Pepperoni."

"It is the greatest! It is the greatest!"
said Pepperoni.